Set in the late 1990's, *Professional Skepticism* takes up a timely matter in its portrayal of four accountants working for a Big Five accounting firm. The jockeying for position, power and money among the audit team is both hysterically funny and scarily dramatic. The team leader is Leo who suffers from emotional and professional disappointment, and tries to remain in a position of authority while his personal life is slipping away. Margaret -- entrenched in the old boys' network -- seeks respect and a deserved promotion, even during character attacks. Greg uses politics, religion and popularity to hide his dark secret from the audit team. And Paul, our naïve hero, struggles to find his place as a new auditor under the cloak of his own private ambitions. Taking place over a four-week period, the Mason Industries' audit scandal will change these characters into today's headline-making personalities.

Professional Skepticism

James Rasheed
Professional Skepticism

© 2022
James Rasheed
Self-publishing
Original Cover Image curtesy of Peter Urban from Boston
Cover and formatting by Chasity Nicole at InkDragon Publishing
© 2022
https://www.facebook.com/groups/530987690664538
ISBN:

Professional Skepticism is dedicated to Ray Sawyer,
my former college professor.

Contents

ORIGINAL PRODUCTION

Professional Skepticism was first produced professionally by the
Wellfleet Harbor Actors Theater in Wellfleet, Massachusetts in 2002.
It was directed by Jason Slavick with the following cast:

LEO .... Robert Pemberton*

PAUL .... Chris Faith*

GREG .... Yaegel Welch*

MARGARET .... Marianna Bassham*

* *Members of Actors Equity Association, the union of professional
actors, stage managers, and choreographers.*

CHARACTERS

LEO: thirty-one, senior accountant

PAUL: twenty-six, a second -year staff accountant, should always be played as a Southerner.

GREG: twenty-three, African-American, a first-year staff accountant.

MARGARET: twenty-eight, a senior accountant

TIME

August 2000.

PLACE

All scenes take place in a conference room in a Big Five accounting firm in Charleston, South Carolina.

PROFESSIONAL SKEPTICISM

by James Rasheed

Professional Skepticism

Scene One

*At rise. Early Tuesday afternoon. Leo is sitting at
the conference table reviewing an audit folder.
Paul and Greg enter.*

PAUL: (*To Greg.*) How about three on Sunday?

GREG: Three? That should give us enough time.

PAUL: If we eat around 12:30, we'll be fine. I'll call in a
few minutes … Leo, have you heard anything else
about the merger?

LEO: (*Annoyed.*) Why didn't you wait on me?

PAUL: We looked for you. Where were you?

LEO: Here.

PAUL: Here, where? I couldn't find you. I thought you
went to lunch with Diane.

LEO: No.

PAUL: Sorry about that.

LEO: Where did you eat?

PAUL: Aaron's Deli.

LEO: Hah.

PAUL: Did you eat?

LEO: No.

PAUL: We didn't leave you on purpose.

LEO: (*To Greg.*) Hand me the accounts-receivable folder.

GREG: It's on the table over there.

PAUL: (*To Leo.*) Are you hungry?

LEO: What?

PAUL: Let me go get you a Coke and some crackers.

LEO: I'll eat tonight.

PAUL: You like those peanut butter crackers.

LEO: Forget it.

PAUL: It's my fault, please.

(Leo doesn't respond.)
PAUL: *(Continues.)* I'm buying you a pack of crackers
        and a Coke … Greg, you want a Coke?
GREG: Sure.
PAUL: Two Cokes and a pack of peanut butter crackers.
        *(Paul scrounges around his area at the table looking
        for money.)*
PAUL: *(Continues. To Greg.)* Lend me a few dollars.
GREG: All I have is a twenty.
PAUL: Do you have any change?
LEO: *(Pulling out his wallet.)* Here. Now go!
        (Paul takes the money.)
PAUL: I'll pay you back tomorrow because this is my
        treat.
LEO: Go!
PAUL: I forgot to run by the money machine this morning.
        (Paul crosses to the door leading to the hallway.)
LEO: *(To Paul.)* Did you leave any audit folders at the
        clients?
PAUL: No. We brought everything back to the office. I
        packed the trunk myself.
LEO: Then where is the inventory folder?
PAUL: *(Crossing back to the table.)* I was using it this
        morning.
        (Paul hands Leo the inventory folder.)
LEO: (Army drill tone.) I want all the folders, in order, in
        the audit trunk.
PAUL: OK.
LEO: I can't find a goddamn thing!
        (Paul starts gathering audit folders.)
LEO: *(Continues.)* What a mess! … This isn't finished.
PAUL: I said I was still working on it.
LEO: What the hell were you doing at the clients? All of
        this should have been done by now.
PAUL: We're on schedule.
LEO: No, we're not.

PAUL: When's our deadline?

LEO: I talked with Luther this morning. The client would like the financials issued on the eighteenth.

PAUL: That's not even three weeks! I'm still waiting on bank confirmations. And accounts receivable confirmations.

LEO: Luther promised the client.

PAUL: There's no way we can issue these financials on the eighteenth. Not with an unqualified opinion. Seventeen days?

LEO: I'm on this audit to speed your ass up.

PAUL: Luther shouldn't have promised Mr. Gilreath anything before consulting with us.

LEO: I told him it wouldn't be a problem.

PAUL: Leo?

LEO: Aren't you going somewhere?

PAUL: Oh yeah. Sorry, Leo.

(Paul exits the room.)

LEO: What are you and pinhead planning on Sunday?

GREG: Racquetball after church.

LEO: Where do you play?

GREG: Paul's a member at Windsor Country Club.

LEO: Windsor? That's a shitty golf course. You play golf … Tiger?

GREG: Yeah. Haven't played around here yet. Paul's not a golfer.

LEO: I wouldn't be hanging out with him. You know what I mean?

GREG: I've been to a driving range a few times.

LEO: Diane and I are members over at Crescent.

GREG: I've heard it's a nice place.

LEO: It is … I can get you in. *(Referring to Greg's race.)* It wouldn't be an issue.

GREG: I'd like to play there.

LEO: Good. This weekend, I'll take you over. Show you the course.

GREG: I can't this weekend. How about next?

LEO: Your loss. So, how do you like it here?

GREG: It's been OK … I really do want to play at
      Crescent.

LEO: We'll see. You getting any?

GREG: What?
      (LEO laughs.)

GREG: *(Continues.)* Leo, pass me the audit manual.

LEO: *(Handing Greg the audit manual.)* How much did
      they start you out at?

GREG: Huh?

LEO: How much are they paying staff accountants this
      year?

GREG: Thirty-eight.
      (Paul enters with a pack of crackers and two Cokes.)

PAUL: *(To Leo.)* There you go. You really shouldn't skip
      lunch. *(To Greg.)* Here Bubba.

GREG: Thanks.

PAUL: *(Pulls out a little pocket notebook and begins
      writing.)* I owe Leo four dollars.

LEO: Greg was telling me they started this year's group
      out at thirty-eight.

PAUL: No way. Last year I started at thirty-four.

LEO: Too bad.

PAUL: They must be adjusting.

LEO: Thirty-four thousand wouldn't pay my grocery bill.

PAUL: Even with my raise this year, I'm not making
      thirty-eight.

LEO: I started around thirty-eight. Four years ago!

PAUL: I'm making enough. It's not like we're living in
      Boston or New York.

LEO: You should have negotiated.

PAUL: I didn't want to negotiate.

LEO: Why not?

PAUL: I wasn't going to mess up my opportunity to work
      for a Big Five accounting firm.

LEO: Luther makes over three hundred thousand a year.
PAUL: None of us want to work for a small firm.
GREG: I wouldn't.
PAUL: Leo, you're always making fun of guys working at
     small firms like Jordan and Company.
LEO: They're all a bunch of losers.
PAUL: You want to hear something worse? A friend of
     mine was let go at Peat. He just accepted a job with
     the IRS.
LEO: Fuck that.
GREG: (*Overlapping.*) No way.
LEO: You sold yourself short.
PAUL: I don't care. Working for Edwin and Wyndham is
     prestigious.
LEO: Whoo wee. They pay us crap.
PAUL: Managers make pretty good money. Eighty
     thousand is decent.
LEO: You have to wait almost five years.
PAUL: I'd be happy with eighty.
LEO: Who says you're going to make it to manager?
PAUL: (*With conviction.*) I'm going to be a partner.
LEO: Bullshit. If this merger goes through, you'll be out
     of here by the end of the month. This place will just
     be a blot on your résumé.
GREG: Leo, what have you heard?
LEO: It's called downsizing. Some of you will be
     "deselected."
     (*Paul pulls out his little pocket notebook.*)
PAUL: Pierce and Hawthorne have twelve staff
     accountants to our ten.
GREG: (*Overlapping.*) They're not going to eight-six any
     of the first-year staff accountants.
LEO: (*Patting Greg on the back.*) Don't let the door hit
     you in the ass on your way out.
PAUL: (*Directed at Leo.*) Well, they also have five
     seniors.

LEO: Stop fucking around and get back to work.

PAUL: (*Quietly.*) Three managers and two partners …
Where's my ruler? Did someone take my ruler?
(Finding his ruler under a stack of folders.) Never
mind.

LEO: Thirty-four thousand. Ha. Oh well.

PAUL: I had other offers. Arthur Anderson in Atlanta
offered me more money and better benefits.

LEO: So?

PAUL: I prefer living here.

LEO: Ahhhh. Pauley likes Charleston. Sweet … So
sweet.

GREG: Leo. Leave him alone.

LEO: (*To Greg.*) I'm surprised you're not living in
Atlanta.

GREG: Why?

LEO: (*Homosexuality reference.*) You just seem like a
Hotlanta kind of guy … Luther originally offered me
thirty-three. I thought to myself, fuck that. I said,
"No, thank you." Then he asked, "What would make
you happy?" *(Lets out a slight laugh.)* What would
make you happy? *(To Paul.)* Too bad you got a
lousy deal.

PAUL: (*To Greg, picking up the phone.*) I'll reserve the
racquetball court for Sunday.

LEO: Guys, I wouldn't make plans for this weekend.
Your butts are in here until this audit is completed.

PAUL: Leo, I have already made plans.

LEO: Team is not spelled with an "I."

GREG: On Sunday, I can't be here until after one.
(To Paul)
You're still planning to go to church with me?

PAUL: Well … We'll talk later.

LEO: Where do you go to church?

GREG: Riverside Baptist. You and Diane should join us.

LEO: (*Laughs.*) No.

PAUL: Leo's Catholic.

GREG: My mother was Catholic … until she was saved.

LEO: You drink?

GREG: Yes.

LEO: It wasn't lemonade you were sipping at the office
      party.

GREG: I drink in moderation.

LEO: But I thought all Baptists abstain from alcohol?

GREG: (*Adamantly.*) That's an ignorant misconception.

LEO: (*Smiling.*) Whoa! … So, it's an ignorant
      misconception? I have missed the boat … Here's
      what I think. You drink, you just hope no one from
      your little church group catches you.

GREG: I have nothing to hide.

LEO: You look like a closet case to me. (*To Paul.*)
      Pauley, I thought you were an Episcopalian. What
      the hell happened? (*Putting a cigarette in his mouth.*)
      Pauley. Pauley. Pauley. You disappoint me, man.
      You're letting Greg drag you to a goddamn fundy
      church.

GREG: Most Baptists are not right-wing fundamentalists.

LEO: (*To Paul.*) You better practice saying, "Praise the
      Lord! … Yes, Jesus! Who wants to come up here and
      be saved … Yes, Jesus."

GREG: (*Overlapping.*) There are extremists in every other
      mainstream Protestant denomination. Including the
      Episcopal church. You are so full of shit.

LEO: I hear you, brother. Let's get fired up. (*Leo picks up
      his crackers and drink. He begins singing Daniel L.
      Schufte's "Here I am, Lord."*) "Here I am, Lord. Is
      it I, Lord? I have heard you calling in the night. I
      will go, Lord, if you lead me. I will hold your people
      in my heart."

PAUL: Just ignore him.

      (*Leo returns to the door.*)

LEO: (*Imitating the television evangelist, Ernest Anglsley.*)
    Amen. Can you say, "Amen?"
    (Leo exits.)
GREG: Asshole … At Sunday school, they say we should
    pray for people like Leo.
PAUL: Right now?
GREG: I'll have his name placed on the prayer list.
PAUL: (*Relieved.*) Oh, good.
GREG: Bud, did you hear about Margaret?
PAUL: What's the matter?
GREG: She received her grades in the mail this morning.
PAUL: Already?
GREG: Yeah.
PAUL: The dreaded CPA exam. How did she do?
GREG: Passed her final two parts.
PAUL: You're kidding! … Thank goodness.
GREG: How many times has she taken the exam?
PAUL: I shouldn't say. *(Pause.)* That's like her seventh
    time.
GREG: Seven times, wow.
PAUL: There will be a party at Margaret's tonight.
GREG: You've already passed the exam, right?
PAUL: Yes. Last year I enrolled in a one-week intensive
    review course in Atlanta and passed all four parts on
    my first try.
GREG: Impressive.
PAUL: Each part has less than a twenty-five percent pass
    rate.
GREG: What were your grades?
PAUL: Seventy-five, seventy-five, seventy-five, and
    seventy-five. The lowest passing grades.
GREG: Hey, you got it over with.
PAUL: Not bad for one week of studying. How do you
    think you did?
GREG: It's in God's hands.
PAUL: Were you prepared?

GREG: I spent a lot of time in prayer.

PAUL: You studied also, didn't you?

GREG: Yeah.

PAUL: You'll do fine. Besides, very few people pass all four parts on their first try. I was fortunate. I wouldn't worry about it.

GREG: I'll know soon.

PAUL: The firm gives you three years to pass the exam. You have plenty of time. So don't worry.

GREG: I guess Leo's passed.

PAUL: (*Looking at the door.*) Not the law section.

GREG: No way.

PAUL: Oh yes. Margaret and Leo usually go out together and get drunk when the grades arrive.

GREG: He's been here over three years?

PAUL: They're keeping him because we've had a high turnover of senior accountants. But they won't promote him to manager until he passes. Leo will have a cow when he finds out Margaret passed. Especially if he screwed up again.

GREG: If he fails this time, will they let him go?

PAUL: Probably.

GREG: Too bad.

PAUL: But Luther will keep him until he finishes up all the audits he's working on. Bubba, if you passed any parts, I'll buy you a beer.

GREG: We'll see.

PAUL: You want to go to Clancy's around nine?

GREG: Let's hope we get out of here by nine.

PAUL: I'm craving Mexican food.

GREG: I may just stay home tonight.

PAUL: Come on.

GREG: No.

PAUL: I'll drive … My treat.

GREG: A Monterey's burrito does sound good.

PAUL: And a couple Margaritas.

GREG: See if Margaret wants to come.
PAUL: I'll give her a call.
GREG: (*Insinuating a sexual relationship.*) Bud, are
      Margaret and Leo …
PAUL: They were.
      (*Leo enters.*)
LEO: Margaret just gave me a copy of the press release.
      Ladies, the merger is official. Come on, Luther wants
      to see all of us now.

Scene Two

*At Rise: Projected on the conference room's white
board: "Mason Industries Audit; Saturday 9:00 AM;
August 5, 2000; Deadline: 13 days." Leo and Greg
are in the room working.*

GREG: You were right about that Ping putter. I tried it out
    at the putting greens during lunch yesterday.
LEO: I was wondering where you were. If you had gotten
    lost.
GREG: The putter has a good feel to it.
LEO: Isn't it great on the fast greens?
GREG: Yeah. Hey, I brought it back. It's in my trunk.
LEO: It's yours.
GREG: Are you sure?
LEO: Did the ball feel smooth coming off the club head?
GREG: Yeah.
LEO: Then just say, "Thank you, Leo."
GREG: Thanks, Leo.
LEO: Besides, I just bought an Odyssey.
GREG: I'm ready to play at Crescent.
LEO: We'll see.
    *(Paul enters with a bag of biscuits. He sets down his
    audit bag and quickly crosses back to the door. Paul
    opens the door and looks down the hall.)*
PAUL: That was odd. I was walking down the hall and
    Luther came out of his office. Just as I was about to
    say, "Good morning," he turned around and went
    back in … Huh. Funny. *(Pause.)* I hate working on
    Saturdays.
LEO: Are you looking for a job or a career?
PAUL: *(Handing out biscuits.)* One sausage and egg
    biscuit for Leo. And Greg wanted ham.

GREG: (*Pulling out a dollar.*) How much do I owe you?

PAUL: Dollar and a half.

GREG: All I've got is a dollar.

PAUL: We'll call it even.

LEO: I'll catch you later.

PAUL: Don't worry about it. (*Paul takes out his pocket notebook and records the cost of Leo's biscuit.*) Any more news about the merger?

GREG: No.

LEO: So, Paul, how are you doing?

PAUL: Great.

LEO: I felt so sorry for you yesterday.

PAUL: Why?

LEO: I'm glad it was you who was up there and not me.

PAUL: My presentation? I thought my presentation went very well.

LEO: Luther understands it was your first time.

PAUL: I covered the topic. What did I leave out? I did a pretty good job.

LEO: Luther can be an asshole.

PAUL: (*With increasing anxiety.*) You think he's disappointed in me? (*Crosses to the door and looks down the hall.*) OK, Luther asked some questions I couldn't answer. I'm going to get back to him on it. All I was supposed to do was present a broad overview. Leo, did he say something to you?

LEO: No. (*Pause.*) I just know Luther.

PAUL: I gave handouts. I used computer-generated special effects in my overheads. Everyone laughed whenever the cartoon accountant ran across the screen. (*Imitating the cartoon accountant.*) "No more FASBS! No more FASBS ..."

LEO: Paul, your cartoon accountant resembled Luther.

PAUL: No, it didn't.

LEO: That's what people are saying.

PAUL: No. You're joking.

LEO: Whatever.

PAUL: Shoot. I was just trying to use the right balance of humor. When you're talking about FASBs … it's pretty dry stuff … No wonder Luther didn't want to talk to me this morning.

LEO: Don't fuck up next time.

PAUL: Shoot! I volunteered to go again next Friday.

LEO: Just stick to your damn topic.

PAUL: How bad was it? … I didn't embarrass myself, though. Did I?

LEO: Huh.

PAUL: Maybe I should speak to Luther. *(Pause.)* No, I don't want to bother him. Especially if he's ticked off. I'll let him calm down. *(To Greg.)* How do you think I did?

GREG: I don't know, I wasn't paying attention.

PAUL: You should pay attention.

GREG: Bud, who cares?

PAUL: Your clients may ask you questions related to those issues.

GREG: Yeah.

PAUL: In a lot of cases, you can save them money.

GREG: What's your topic for next week?

PAUL: Fraud. Preventing and investigating fraud. I'm discussing the "fraud triangle" of opportunity, motivation, and rationalization. I was planning on using a cartoon character that looks like an accountant dressed as Sherlock Holmes. *(Pause.)* I gave a decent presentation, didn't I?

LEO: GODDAMN IT, FORGET ABOUT IT!

PAUL: OK. Sorry. Anyway, I don't care.

GREG: *(Picking up his coffee cup.)* I need another cup of coffee.

 (Greg walks out of the room.)

LEO: What did y'all do last night?

PAUL: Same as usual. Greg and I went to Clancy's. Half
        of the office showed up. Where were you and Diane?
LEO: We stayed in.
PAUL: I haven't seen Diane in weeks.
LEO: Who was the band?
PAUL: Doppelganger is playing again this weekend. We
        didn't leave Clancy's until after two. We left
        Margaret dancing on top of a table. Totally plastered.
LEO: What do you think about Greg acing the CPA exam?
PAUL: WHAT?
LEO: Luther was telling me this morning that Greg made
        the third highest grades in the state. High nineties on
        all four parts. Can you believe that? High nineties.
        Ninety-seven on auditing. Law, he made a ninety-
        eight. *(Trying to recall.)* Accounting and reporting?
        He made a ninety …
PAUL: *(Quickly.)* I've always heard if you make over a
        seventy-five, you've studied too much.
LEO: Accounting and reporting, he made a ninety-six. He
        didn't do so well on that one.
PAUL: It really doesn't matter if you make a seventy-five
        or a hundred. Who gives a darn?
LEO: Luther invited him to lunch on Wednesday.
PAUL: Good for Greg.
LEO: Good for Greg. Luther wants to show him off.
        They're going to hold on to him. Greg's the next
        superstar. I just have a gut feeling he is.
PAUL: Greg's a great guy. We're good friends.
LEO: I wouldn't be surprised if he makes partner in less
        than ten years. He's the next David McClain.
PAUL: Who?
LEO: David McClain is in the Charlotte office. He made
        partner in only eight and a half years. Yeah, just like
        David McClain, Greg's a superstar. Super. Star.
        Third highest in the state. Grades make a big
        difference.

(Pause.)
PAUL: Are you taking the exam again in November?
LEO: No.
PAUL: You passed? *(Pause.)* Leo?
LEO: I haven't received my grades yet.
PAUL: But everyone else has … I'd call the postmaster.
LEO: I don't give a shit.
PAUL: If you didn't pass this time, won't you lose credit
     for all the other parts? You'd have to take the whole
     exam over again.
LEO: It's not your fucking concern.
PAUL: You can have my old study guides. I don't need
     them.
LEO: Has Luther ever taken you to lunch?
     (Greg enters.)
PAUL: No.
GREG: Sorry. Luther cornered me again. He wanted to
     know how the audit was going. Asked about the two
     of you.
PAUL: What did he say about me?
GREG: He kept calling you Peter.
PAUL: Shoot … Did he say anything else about the
     merger?
LEO: Yes. When the merger's completed, Peter is the first
     to be fired.
GREG: Leo, I'm taking a long lunch on Wednesday.
LEO: I don't know. We have a lot of work to finish.
GREG: Luther approved it.
LEO: *(Looking at Paul.)* Did he?
     (Paul stands up and crosses to Greg.)
PAUL: *(Shaking Greg's hand.)* Congratulations on acing
     the exam.
GREG: Thanks.
PAUL: You should have called me.
GREG: It's no big deal.

PAUL: When we go to Clancy's tonight, I'll buy you a
	couple of beers.
GREG: We'll see.
PAUL: I think it's fantastic.
GREG: (*To Paul.*) Margaret just walked in. Go see how
	pale she looks.
PAUL: I can't believe she made it in this morning.
GREG: She's making everyone who was there last night
	swear to secrecy.
PAUL: (*To Leo.*) We were all doing shots. (*To Greg.*) I
	stopped after what? Three? With Margaret, we quit
	counting. She was hanging all over one of the guys in
	the band.
	(*Margaret enters.*)
MARGARET: Good morning, sweethearts.
PAUL: Morning, Margaret.
GREG: (*Overlapping.*) Good morning.
MARGARET: (*Deadpan.*) Hey, Leo.
LEO: Did you have fun last night?
MARGARET: You should have been there.
LEO: Why don't you jump on top of the table and show
	me what I missed.
	(*Paul lowers his head.*)
MARGARET: Leo, why don't you go fuck a tree?
	(*Margaret crosses to Paul.*) Big mouth.
PAUL: I'm so sorry … I casually mentioned something
	about last night …
MARGARET: (*Fixing Paul's collar.*) Darling, hold still.
PAUL: Sorry … Thank you.
	(*Leo slams the door shut.*)
MARGARET: (*To Paul, rubbing her temples.*) Aspirin,
	honey. Aspirin.
PAUL: (*Spastically.*) I have a whole bottle. Hold on a
	second.
	(*Paul reaches into his audit bag for a bottle of
	aspirin.*)

MARGARET: (*To Paul, referring to his biscuit.*) Mmmm.
     Something smells good. Let me have a little tiny bite.
PAUL: (*Eagerly.*) Please! Eat! Eat!
     (*Margaret takes a bite.*)
LEO: Would you like a Bloody Mary to go with your
     biscuit?
     (*Margaret makes a gesture at Leo.*)
PAUL: (*Out of breath, handing the bottle to Margaret.*)
     There you go.
MARGARET: You're so sweet.
PAUL: I live to serve.
     (*Margaret takes some aspirin.*)
MARGARET: Greg, when are we working together?
GREG: You tell me.
MARGARET: I have an audit coming up next month in
     Myrtle Beach.
PAUL: I want to go.
MARGARET: Three weeks on the beach.
PAUL: Request me.
MARGARET: I'll talk with Mike and Rob this morning.
     They're working on the new schedule.
PAUL: We would have so much fun.
GREG: Give me a call.
LEO: Margaret in a hotel room with two boys. That
     wouldn't be the first time.
MARGARET: (*To Leo.*) Sounds like you're not getting
     any. Diane cut you off again?
     (*Leo lets out a slight laugh.*)
MARGARET: (*Continues.*) She wouldn't let you come to
     my party the other night? We had fun without you
     anyway. (*To Greg.*) I'm glad you were there. (*To
     Leo.*) What does Diane want this time?
     (*Leo ignores her.*)
MARGARET: (*Continues.*) He's a moody bastard when
     she cuts him off.

PAUL: Margaret, have you heard anything new about the
       merger?
MARGARET: Oh God, yes. We're moving into Pierce
       and Hawthorne's building.
       (Leo throws down the audit folder he's reviewing.)
PAUL: They're down on Calhoun Street.
GREG: When are we moving?
MARGARET: End of next month.
PAUL: We have the prime location.
MARGARET: They have more office space.
LEO: I knew this would happen. They'll have the home-
       court advantage.
PAUL: Parking is horrible on Calhoun Street.
LEO: PARKING? You moron, don't you see what's
       going on? When they start laying off, our office will
       have the most casualties.
PAUL: You think?
MARGARET: *(To Paul.)* They're not going to fire you.
       (Hugging Paul.) Honey, everyone loves you. You're
       such a sweetie. *(Indicating a headache.)* Shit, I've
       got work to do. *(Crossing to the door.)* I'll let y'all
       know about Myrtle Beach.
GREG: Great.
PAUL: Sounds exciting.
MARGARET: *(Breathlessly.)* Oh God, yes. Call me for
       lunch.
GREG: I will.
PAUL: *(Overlapping.)* I will.
MARGARET: *(Flirtatiously.)* Bye, Leo. I hope Diane lets
       you come out and play some time.
       (Margaret exits.)
GREG: Margaret's wild.
PAUL: She's a hoot. Did you see her taking shots of that
       stuff that looked like cement?
GREG: Yeah.

PAUL: It looked nasty. I wouldn't touch it … She'll drink
    anything.
LEO: Shoe polish?
PAUL: (*Jokingly.*) If you put it in a shot glass.
LEO: Paul, what are you saying?
PAUL: What do you mean?
LEO: … You think Margaret has a problem?
PAUL: No.
LEO: You just said she'd drink shoe polish.
PAUL: It was a joke.
LEO: Weird sense of humor calling someone an alcoholic.
PAUL: I didn't say that.
LEO: You implied it.
PAUL: (*Frustrated.*) NO! I wasn't implying Margaret's
    an alcoholic.
LEO: What a thing to say!
PAUL: I didn't ---
LEO: Just shut up.
    (*Silence.*)
PAUL: (*Looking through an audit folder.*) Greg, do you
    have a second?
GREG: Yeah.
PAUL: Did you go back and investigate any of these
    differences?
GREG: No.
PAUL: But I thought we talked about this.
GREG: The audit program says to investigate differences
    greater than ten thousand dollars. If it's less than ten
    thousand, it's I.N.F.E., Immaterial ---
PAUL: Immaterial, no further investigation. I know that.
    But you have to look at your overall results. There
    are numerous differences in the eight- and nine-
    thousand-dollar range. That's why I told you to
    perform additional procedures.
GREG: (*Handing Paul the audit program.*) Read the audit
    program.

PAUL: I know what the audit program says.

GREG: Well, if you followed the audit program, you wouldn't be going over the time budgets in your areas.

PAUL: But you also have to use your common sense. First of all, Leo wrote the audit program. *(To Leo.)* No offense, Leo.

LEO: What are you girls bitching about?

PAUL: Leo, I have a question. *(Showing Leo, the audit program.)* How did you calculate this number?

LEO: I didn't. It's the same figure they used in the prior year.

PAUL: So, who calculated it?

LEO: What's your problem?

PAUL: Look at these work papers. See how many differences there are in the eight- and nine-thousand-dollar range?

LEO: So, what?

PAUL: Luther is not going to sign off on these work papers. One of us will have to go back on site and perform additional procedures.

LEO: If Luther wants these financials issued in a week and a half, he'll sign off on the goddamn work papers.

PAUL: How can he?

LEO: Luther brought this client in twelve years ago. He and Mr. Gilreath go to church together. They're golfing buddies … This is Luther's audit! And you're not going to fuck it up for all of us.

PAUL: It's still not right.

LEO: You know what your problem is?

PAUL: What?

LEO: You can't see the forest for the trees.

PAUL: Why do we even attempt to audit? We should just write I.N.F.I. on all the work papers. Maybe Katherine can order us an I.N.F.I. stamp. *(Flipping through one of the folders and pretending to stamp the pages.)* Immaterial, no further investigation. *(As he's flipping pages.)* Immaterial. Immaterial. Immaterial. Immaterial. Immaterial. Immat---

LEO: You better remember, I'm giving you a performance evaluation on this audit. I'll remember this when I do.

PAUL: And another thing, I don't like the fact that we've been given an unrealistic deadline.

LEO: Hey … I don't give a fuck.

PAUL: Who runs the audit? Us? Or the client?

LEO: *(Holding up an audit folder.)* I still can't figure out what the hell you were doing while you were at Mason Industries. Jerking off?

PAUL: Maybe you should have come on site more than once. *(Pause.)* I'm documenting our conversation.

LEO: *(Lets out a slight laugh.)* Go ahead. I don't give a fuck.

PAUL: According to the audit manual, both you and Luther will have to sign off on it. *(Pause.)* Leo, I'm serious.

LEO: You're just screwing yourself.

PAUL: I'm following the audit manual. *(Reading from the audit manual.)* "When there are disagreements among the audit team … those differences should be documented and signed off by the ---"

LEO: No one does that shit! We're in the middle of a goddamn merger. Do you really want to be labeled a troublemaker?

PAUL: You're putting us at risk. *(To Greg.)* I'm not angry with you. I realize you're still learning. I won't mention you in the work paper. *(With increasing intensity.)* But the next time I give you an audit note, you better do it. If you don't understand why, ask me.

(Paul begins typing on his laptop. Leo stands behind him reading over his shoulder.)

LEO: I'll remember this … Greg, on Monday you're going
     back to Mason Industries.
GREG: I was following your audit program.
LEO: (*Throwing the folder to Greg.*) Talk to your buddy!
     Investigate any differences over $5,000.
GREG: (*To Paul.*) Thanks, Bud!
LEO: (*To Paul.*) Does that get you off? On Monday
     morning, call the controller and let him know that
     pretty boy is coming back to blow him one more
     time.

Scene Three

At rise: Projected on the white board --- "Same day, 10:30 PM" Leo and Greg are sitting together chatting. Paul, separating himself from the others, sits at the opposite end of the room and works on an audit folder.

GREG: (*Laughing.*) No way.
LEO: (*Enjoying his own company.*) So, my frat brother, Bill, is daring me to fuck her. Hell, it would be a boost for her ego. For me, it's better than beating off. I take her back to the house. We get there. She tells me she's having her period.
(*Paul cringes with disgust.*)
LEO: (*Continues.*) Fuck! … So, I fuck her on Bill's bed.
(*Phone rings. Leo crosses to phone.*)
LEO: (*Continues. On phone.*) Hello … What? … Diane, I told you we're working late.
PAUL: (*Overlapping.*) HI, DIANE!
LEO: We have a deadline coming up. (*Pause.*) I don't have time to talk … I'm too busy … NO. We're not going tomorrow … I'm working …Diane, if you want to go, then go … I'll be home in about an hour … You know, it's up to you. (*Hanging up the phone.*) Fuck her! (*Pause.*) Diane never things about me. It's always what she wants. (*Pause.*) If she goes, I'll never forgive her.
(*Paul begins packing up his things.*)
LEO: (*Continues.*) When this audit is over, I'm going out and getting me some strange. (*Challenging Paul.*) You coming with me? Get you some strange … When's the last time you got laid?
PAUL: I'm going home.

LEO: We still have another hour.
PAUL: We've been here since nine this morning.
     (Defiantly.) Leo, I've finished what I'm working on.
     I'm tired and I'm going home.
LEO: See if Greg needs any help.
PAUL: Greg, you need any help?
GREG: No.
PAUL: *(To Greg.)* You want to come over and watch a
     movie?
GREG: No.
PAUL: We could do your laundry at my place.
LEO: Greg wants to finish his work.
PAUL: I bought some Guinness. Your favorite.
LEO: I'm hungry. I could go for a pizza. Greg, I know
     you could go for some pizza. *(Pause.)* Pizza, pizza?
     (Pause.)
GREG: Yeah.
LEO: Paul, go pick up a pizza. *(To Greg.)* Call in an
     extra-large pepperoni.
     (Greg picks up the phone and dials.)
PAUL: Where could I charge the time?
LEO: Charge it to miscellaneous.
PAUL: I already have thirty-two hours in miscellaneous.
LEO: Look on the time sheet, there's a category called
     administration. Put it there.
PAUL: In ADMINISTRATION? … No. No. It isn't
     right. I'll eat the time before I charge it there.
GREG: *(On phone.)* Pick up … One extra-large pepperoni

PAUL: And mushrooms … Shoot!
GREG: *(On phone.)* And mushrooms … Paul. Thanks.
PAUL: *(To Leo.)* Give me the money first.
LEO: Here's a twenty. I want my change.
GREG: About fifteen minutes.
     *(Paul sits in the corner and pouts. Silence. Margaret
     enters.)*

MARGARET: Come on boys, we're heading to Clancy's.
PAUL: Leo says no.
MARGARET: Leo! Go home and face Diane.
LEO: Fly away. We're working.
    (Margaret picks up a folder and glances through it.)
MARGARET: How far along are you?
LEO: Don't touch anything!
MARGARET: OK. I love hard-working men. *(To Paul.)*
    See you at Clancy's. No wimping out on us. *(To
    Greg.)* You're still coming?
GREG: I have to get up early for church.
MARGARET: Come on. Stay for thirty minutes.
    (Grabbing Greg's hands.) You're my shagging
    partner.
    (Margaret and Greg begin to dance.)
MARGARET: *(Continues.)* Greg, don't be like Leo. He
    doesn't like us anymore.
GREG: I'll come down for one drink.
MARGARET: Dip me Darlin'!
PAUL: My turn! My turn! My turn!
LEO: Paul, go get the pizza!
PAUL: I'm going! I'm going! I'm going!
LEO: Pauley!
PAUL: WHAT?
LEO: Grab a twelve pack, too.
    *(Paul, as he's exiting, pulls out his pocket notebook to
    write down the beer.)*
GREG: Are we on for Myrtle Beach?
MARGARET: Not yet, Goddamnit. I'm still working on
    it.
    (Leo let's out a slight laugh.)
MARGARET: *(Continues. To Greg.)* You and Rob are
    scheduled for the medical university. Mike has Paul
    running the Carolina Federal Bank audit ... Paul is
    becoming our bank audit specialist.
LEO: Big deal! Banks are basically tick-mark audits.

MARGARET: There's a little more to it than that.

GREG: Sounds boring.

LEO: They're so goddamn regulated. Easy audits.

MARGARET: With the merger going through, Paul has found his niche.

LEO: Whoo wee.

MARGARET: Leo, have you ever been on a bank audit?

LEO: They only assign bank audits to pinheads.

MARGARET: You are so full of shit.

LEO: Darling, that's why my eyes are brown.

GREG: Huh … Poor Paul.

MARGARET: What?

GREG: (*Hesitantly.*) Paul was telling me; he really hates auditing banks. Had a real bad experience on the last one. Now he can't stand them.
(Leo suddenly stops what he's doing and looks at Greg.)

MARGARET: Oh, my God.

GREG: He was worried Mike would put him on that audit … Paul already thinks Luther hates him.

MARGARET: Should I say something to Mike?

GREG: Hey, don't get me involved. I'm serious.

MARGARET: I'll talk with Mike. *(Exiting the room.)* Oh well … See you at Clancy's.
(Greg continues to work on his folder. Leo stares at him.)

Scene Four

*Setting: Projected on the white board "Mason
Industries Audit; Friday 2:45 PM; August 18, 2000;
Deadline: 7 Days." The room is empty. An excited
Paul enters and dances around the room. A few
moments later Leo and Greg enter.*

LEO: That was a total waste of time.
PAUL: No, it wasn't.
LEO: Were you wearing that tie as a joke?
PAUL: Hah!
GREG: Bud, if you want to be a partner, dress like a
    partner.
PAUL: (*To Greg; sincerely.*) How do you think I dress?
LEO: Like a manager at the Piggly Wiggly.
GREG: (*To Paul.*) Work on the image, Bud. God helps
    those who help themselves.
PAUL: (*Defensively.*) You can't tell me this time Luther
    wasn't impressed with my presentation.
    (*Silence.*)
PAUL: (*Continues.*) It didn't hurt that I went after Susan.
    I bet you she didn't read the FASB, until this
    morning. Totally unprepared. (*Imitating Susan.*)
    Um. Um. Um. FASB, um. Says um. Um. Um.
    (*Normal voice.*) I counted. She said "um" fifty-seven
    times. I didn't say "um" once. (*To Greg.*) So, what
    did you think?
GREG: Luther didn't seem interested.
PAUL: I saw him taking notes.
GREG: He was writing out his schedule for next week.
PAUL: This time I answered every one of his questions.
GREG: You did better last time.

PAUL: I did not! Did you hear Luther try to stump me with, "What should the CPA do to make sure his work remains privileged?" All fraud investigations should be performed at the direction of the client's attorney. Clearly mark the work papers as "attorney work product." Thank you very much.
(Paul picks up a piece of paper and crosses to the door.)

PAUL: *(Continues.)* I hope they fixed the copier. I was incredible! *(Exiting.)* *(Outside the door, Paul sees Margaret. She is carrying birthday balloons. Paul drags her into the room.)*

PAUL: *(Continues. To Margaret.)* Did you like my presentation?

MARGARET: You were divine … What a lovely tie.

PAUL: Thanks.
(Paul exits. Margaret turns to leave.)

LEO: *(Calling out.)* Margaret! … Margaret.

MARGARET: What?

LEO: Dinner tonight?

MARGARET: *(Taken off guard, awkwardly.)* YES. I'm starving already. Great … Mike is getting the gang together for dinner at Hyman's Seafood.

LEO: No.
(Pause.)

MARGARET: Where did you want to eat?

LEO: Forget it.

MARGARET: Leo, why are you so … YOU? *(To Greg.)* Hey, sweetie.
(Greg looks up and smiles. They exchange hand waves. Margaret exits.)

LEO: *(Reviewing a folder.)* Sweetie, take this folder down to Robin in the tax department. Tell her I will need the tax return by Tuesday.

GREG: So, what are your plans?

LEO: What?

GREG: Paul was saying that since you didn't pass the law
        section you would probably be leaving soon.
        (Margaret enters the doorway.)
MARGARET: Leo, I'm not having dinner with you
        tonight.
LEO: *(To Margaret.)* I said forget about it. *(To Greg,
        handing him the folder.)* Take this to Robin.
PAUL: *(To Margaret; eagerly.)* What are you working on?
MARGARET: *(Walking away.)* I have a three o'clock
        meeting with Luther.
PAUL: I just spoke with Luther in the kitchen …Tell me if
        he says anything about me.
GREG: Was the copier working?
PAUL: It's being serviced again. *(Trying to lighten the
        atmosphere.)* I wish I could get serviced as many
        times a month as the copier does.
        *(Greg leaves the room. Leo takes Paul's piece of
        cake.)*
PAUL: *(Continues.)* I asked Luther if he would like to
        have lunch sometime. He said, "no."
LEO: No?
PAUL: No.
LEO: Just, no?
PAUL: Yes.
LEO: *(Laughing.)* The last person Luther hated isn't even
        in accounting anymore. He's selling life insurance.
PAUL: Shoot!
LEO: If I were you, I would get out. You don't have a
        future with this firm. *(Handing Paul, a business
        card.)* Here's the number of a headhunter who's a
        friend of mine. Send him a copy of your résumé.
        (Pause.) You should do it today.
PAUL: But I like it here!
LEO: During my orientation, one of the managers told us
        to imagine our hand in a bucket of water. Now pull
        your hand out. Look in the bucket. Is there a big

hole where your hand was? NO! Think how quickly
the water fills in. That's how important you are to
this firm. They don't give a fuck about you. *(Pause.)*
Paul, I know for a fact Luther has a list of first- and
second-year staff accountants he has to lay off.

PAUL: But I've been given the responsibilities of a senior.
I'm moving up … I'm a senior, except for the title.

LEO: Hey, Pierce and Hawthorne dictates what goes on
now. They call him up and say, "Luther, reduce your
staff by blank number." The number is out of his
hands.

PAUL: I've already passed the CPA exam. He'll take ---

LEO: And you know Luther is going to start with people
he hates.

PAUL: Have you seen this list? *(Pause.)* Leo?

LEO: WHAT?

PAUL: Am I on this list?

LEO: It wouldn't be my place to tell you.

PAUL: But you know?

LEO: I have no idea who's on the list.

PAUL: I don't believe you.

LEO: Hey, leave me out of this.

PAUL: I'll ask Margaret.

    (Pause.)

LEO: *(Featherlike tone.)* Pauley, my friend, let's be
honest. You're not partner material … It's not just
the suits. You don't have that kill instinct.

PAUL: Yes, I do.

LEO: No, you don't. You're too goddamn nice to be an
auditor.

PAUL: I can be tough.

LEO: Rambo, your clients send you thank-you notes and
birthday cards.

PAUL: I maintain a professional rapport with my clients.

LEO: OK. But you're a … pinhead. You can't change
      that … One client caught you on a security tape
      dancing alone in the elevator.
PAUL: I was doing morning stretches.
LEO: Luther showed us the tape. You were dancing.
      (Greg enters.)
GREG: Robin's not very friendly.
LEO: She's a bitch.
GREG: I asked her when her baby was due and she ---
LEO: WHAT?
PAUL: Oh no! *(Overlapping.)*
      (Leo lets out a hearty laugh.)
LEO: Robin had a little boy about five months ago.
GREG: I thought she was pregnant.
LEO: What did she say? God, I wish I had been there …
      You won't be working in the tax department.
PAUL: *(Overlapping.)* I'm so sorry.
GREG: Shut up. SHUT UP! Just shut up!
LEO: When's it due? Goddamn that cracks me up.
      *(Paul searches on top of and under the table for his
      missing pencil.)*
PAUL: Who stole my mechanical pencil: *(Still searching.)*
      I had it this morning. It's a blue Berol. Leo, did you
      take my pencil?
LEO: I don't need your goddamn pencil … Greg, did
      Robin say she'll have the tax return ready by
      Tuesday?
PAUL: *(Becoming more frustrated.)* I bought it! It's my
      pencil!
GREG: *(Holding up a mechanical pencil.)* Is this it?
PAUL: Yes.
GREG: Don't leave your shit in my space.
PAUL: I'm sorry.
      *(Greg throws the pencil like a dart at Paul. Paul has
      to avoid being hit.)*
PAUL: *(Continues.)* Thanks!

GREG: (*To Leo.*) Robin will have it to you on Thursday.

LEO: That's unacceptable! Go tell her I want the goddamn tax return on my desk, Tuesday morning!
(*Greg does not reply. Leo crumples up a piece of paper and hits Greg in the head with it.*)

GREG: NO!
(*Leo jumps out of his chair and crosses to Greg. Greg immediately stands up.*)

LEO: (*In his face.*) You're a pussy!

GREG: We have an assault. Would you like to try for a battery?

LEO: Fuck you.
(*Leo walks out of the room.*)

PAUL: (*Reviewing a folder.*) Greg, the change in their stock price is not immaterial.
(*Paul cautiously slides the folder to Greg.*)

GREG: Leo signed off on it.
(*Greg slides the folder back to Paul.*)

PAUL: I know, but … Consider the percentage change in their stock price.
(*Paul slides the folder back to Greg. Pause.*) Greg.

GREG: You're not my boss.
(*Greg slides the folder back to Paul.*)

PAUL: Stock manipulation is a possibility here … I'm trying to teach you.

GREG: (*Threatening.*) I've already surpassed you.
(*Leo enters.*)

LEO: WHO WEE! I LIT A FIRE UNDER HER BIG ASS! Robin will have the tax return to me on Monday morning. That's how a man handles things.
(*Laughing.*) "Greg told us you're having twins."

PAUL: (*To Leo.*) The change in their stock price is not immaterial. We should investigate. Look at the equity folder.

LEO: (*Firmly.*) Did I sign off on the work papers?
(*Pause.*)

PAUL: Yes.

LEO: (*Grabbing the folder.*) I forbid. I fucking dare you
to touch any audit folders I don't personally hand
you.
(*Paul jumps up. Leo places him back in the chair.
Paul stands up again. Leo, pushing down on Paul's
head, once again places Paul back in the chair. Paul
quickly stands up again and moves away. Paul eyes
the audit trunk.*)

LEO: (*Continues.*) Don't you touch that audit trunk …
Paul.
(*Paul slowly crosses to the audit trunk.*)

LEO: (*Continues.*) Don't you touch that audit trunk.
(*Pause.*) Paul. Paul. Don't you touch that audit
trunk. Paul!
(*Paul slams down the top of the trunk. He opens it
and slams it again. Paul starts taking audit folders
out of the trunk. Leo crosses to Paul. Leo grabs
Paul, causing the folders in Paul's hands to go flying
across the room. Leo then pins Paul on the top of the
trunk.*)

PAUL: Get off me … Get off me!

LEO: Poor baby. Go whine to Luther. Be a snitch. That
will really help your moron image. (*Releasing Paul.*)
I'm working with twiddle dee and twiddle dumb ass.

GREG: (*To Leo.*) Man, you are fucked!

LEO: (*Quickly.*) Greg, who was that girl you were with the
other night at Garibaldi's? … Girlfriend? She looked
like the little girl in accounting at Mason Industries.

PAUL: Pam? (*To Greg.*) You went on a date with Pam?

GREG: We had dinner.

PAUL: ALONE? You can't date the client … Oh my
goodness, are you SLEEPING WITH HER?

GREG: It's not an issue.

PAUL: It violates the rules of "independence." This whole
    audit is in jeopardy. … Technically, we should
    withdraw from the engagement.
LEO: (*Smiling.*) Luther put together quite a team here. It
    looks like we're all fucked … MAN.
    (*The phone rings. Leo picks up.*)
LEO: (*Continues. On phone.*) Garden club … Hold on,
    Mikey.
PAUL: (*Overlapping.*) An accountant must also be
    independent in appearance.
LEO: (*To Paul.*) Princess.
GREG: We went out one time. I'm not seeing her again.
    (*Leo starts to hand the receiver to Paul and then he
    pulls it away. He does this several times.*)
PAUL: (*To Greg.*) You didn't sleep with her?
GREG: NO!
PAUL: (*To Leo; as he's grabbing for the phone.*) Hand me
    the damn phone! (*On phone.*) Paul speaking …
    Mike, I love auditing banks. Who said I didn't like
    auditing banks? She said that? (*To Greg; covering
    the receiver.*) What did you tell Margaret?
GREG: (*Overlapping.*) I was joking. I was joking.
PAUL: (*On phone.*) …No. Please schedule me for that
    audit. I love banks. I don't know why Greg said that
    to Margaret. Mike, you know I love auditing banks
    … Thanks for calling. Put me on as many bank
    audits as you can. Thanks again … Bye. (*Hangs up
    phone; to Greg.*) Why did you say ---
GREG: I was joking.
PAUL: I don't understand ---
GREG: I WAS JOKING!
LEO: He was obviously joking.
    (*Paul takes two deep breaths.*)
PAUL: Banks are easy.
    (*Paul screams and then lays his head down on the
    table.*)

LEO: What the fuck! … Paul, what the hell are you
      working on?
      *(Paul slides all the folders in his area to Leo. Some
      of them fall off the table.)*
PAUL: I need to lie down.
LEO: Get the hell out of here. You're fucking useless!
PAUL: I'll take my name off this audit. I'll take my name
      off.
LEO: Go home. You look like shit.
PAUL: (*Referring to the audit.*) Yes, I will! YES, I
      WILL! I'll take my name off this audit. *(Violently
      packing his audit bag.)* Banks are easy to audit
      because they're so regulated. They have to keep
      everything in perfect order. WHO WOULDN'T
      WANT TO RUN A BANK AUDIT?
      (Paul crosses to the door. Margaret enters.)
MARGARET: (*To Paul; extremely hostile.*) We need to
      talk!
PAUL: WHAT'S THE MATTER?
MARGARET: WHY ARE YOU TELLING EVERYONE
      I'M AN ALCOHOLIC?
PAUL: WHAT?
MARGARET: Luther's concerned about me, you little
      fucker!
PAUL: Who said that I said that?
MARGARET: Do I drink any more than Mike or Leo?
      Hell, no!
PAUL: (*Overlapping.*) Margaret … I … I … Let me
      explain. Whatever you heard was taken out of
      context. I've never said anything against you. They
      can tell you I haven't.
LEO: (*Enjoying the moment.*) What are you talking about?
MARGARET: (*To Paul.*) You're just like the rest of them.
      Another little prick.
PAUL: No … I'm not. Really, Margaret … I'm a feminist
      at heart. Why don't we go somewhere nice? Just the

two of us and talk. We'll work this out. We've
    always had a special relationship.
MARGARET: "Special?" What do you mean special? …
    You don't? … No. You don't think I would ever date
    you? … Oh, my God. *(Laughs.)* You are a dumb
    fuck.
PAUL: Can we talk?
MARGARET: Go to HELL!
    (Margaret storms out. Paul screams.)
PAUL: Margaret, please listen …
GREG: *(To Paul; realizing an opportunity.)* Bud, you
    shouldn't start rumors. *(Hurries out of the room.)*
    MARGARET! … Margaret, wait.
LEO: Do you sit down to pee?
PAUL: It's a misunderstanding.
LEO: I'd tell you to turn in your balls, but that would be
    assuming you had some.
    (Paul lowers himself into a chair.)
LEO: *(Continues.)* Madonna, what are you doing over
    there? *(Picks up the stock folder.)* The equity folder
    has been completed. *(Throwing it at Paul.)* Now file
    it back and clean up the mess you've made around
    here.
    *(Leo lets out a hearty laugh. Leo exits. Paul picks up
    the equity folder and looks through the work papers.
    After a moment, he places the folder in his audit bag.)*
PAUL: *(Grinning.)* I'll show them all.

END OF ACT 1

Professional Skepticism

Scene One

MARGARET: Where's the little shit? Paul begged me to
    meet him here this morning.
GREG: He's late.
MARGARET: This is unacceptable.
GREG: Now that you're a manager, do something about it.
MARGARET: Who told you I made manager?
GREG: I ran into Mike in the hall. Congratulations.
MARGARET: I had to threaten to quit.
GREG: Really?
MARGARET: Friday afternoon I gave my two-week's
    notice.
GREG: You were pretty upset.
MARGARET: Damn right I was. Luther called me
    Saturday morning and offered me the promotion.
GREG: I'm proud of you.
    *(Greg starts massaging Margaret's shoulders. She
    abruptly pulls away.)*
GREG: *(Continues.)* You're tense.
MARGARET: Greg, you can't be doing that.
GREG: Whoa, OK, Sorry … When are we working
    together?
MARGARET: Soon.
GREG: Let's go out tonight and celebrate.
MARGARET: I'm having dinner with Mike and his wife.
    (Pause.) Why don't you join us?
GREG: You and Mike are managers … Are you sure you
    want to be seen with a lowly staff accountant?

MARGARET: Don't be silly.

GREG: It's just that I don't want to overstep my boundaries.

(Margaret focuses again on Paul. Greg crosses to the table and starts looking through a folder.)

GREG: *(Continues.)* This is not what I expected.

MARGARET: What?

GREG: Nothing, I'm just frustrated.

MARGARET: *(Looking at her watch.)* I'll give Paul five more minutes.

GREG: *(looking through the folder.)* Fuck … Everything is sink or swim. *(Holding up notes.)* Constant criticism. This is bullshit.

MARGARET: They're just jealous.

GREG: Margaret, please put me on your next audit. I could learn so much from you.

MARGARET: I'll see what I can do.

GREG: Leo's no help to me. I hate coming into work.

MARGARET: Things will work out.

GREG: Maybe God doesn't want me here.

PAUL: *(Offstage.)* Did you have a nice weekend? … Good to hear it.

GREG: I'm ready to quit.

MARGARET: No, you're not quitting.

GREG: Then let me work with you!

(Paul reaches the door of the conference room.)

PAUL: *(Offstage; opening the door.)* How about them Braves yesterday?

VOICE: *(Offstage.)* They lost.

PAUL: They'll kick butt next time. *(Paul enters with his reinvented look. His glasses are gone. His hair is slicked back and he's wearing a new suit with a red power tie and red socks. His fashionable appearance is not quite appropriate for an accountant.)* Margaret … Greg.

*(Silence. Both Margaret and Greg have to turn away
to keep from laughing.)*
PAUL: (*Continues.*) Margaret, I'm glad you came. I was
hoping we could talk for a few minutes … alone? …
Please, Greg.
MARGARET: (*To Greg.*) Go on … We're on for tonight?
GREG: Yeah, I guess.
(Margaret crosses to Greg.)
MARGARET: (*To Greg.*) Go to my office. We'll talk.
(Greg picks up his coffee cup and exits the room.)
PAUL: First of all, congratulations! Manager. Wow!
MARGARET: No thanks to you.
PAUL: Luther wasn't going to lose a great auditor like
yourself.
MARGARET: Whatever.
PAUL: Can we get past this misunderstanding between us?
MARGARET: Paul, you don't know when to keep your
big mouth shut.
PAUL: Did you listen to all the messages I left on your
voice mail?
MARGARET: Yes. All fourteen.
PAUL: I come bearing gifts.
*(Paul pulls out one red rose. Margaret doesn't take
the flower. Paul lays it on her lap.)*
PAUL: (*Continues. Reaching into a bag.*) This is to
celebrate your promotion … It's your favorite.
(Pulling out a large bottle of Absolut Vodka.)
Absolut … Not the cheap stuff. (*Realizing.*) Forgive
me for being such a poop head.
MARGARET: (*Angrily.*) No.
PAUL: I don't want this to affect our professional
relationship.
MARGARET: It won't.
PAUL: Because I really need your expertise right now.
MARGARET: What is it?
(Paul pulls out a typed document.)

PAUL: This is strictly confidential. Leo would freak out if he knew I was sharing this with you. It cannot leave this room. Greg doesn't even know about it.

MARGARET: Paul, what?

Pal: Leo and I have uncovered fraud in the Mason Industry audit.

MARGARET: FRAUD?

PAUL: (*Quieting her down.*) Yes. Yes. Yes …

MARGARET: (*Overlapping.*) What kind of fraud?

PAUL: Stock manipulation by Mr. Gilreath and the company's treasurer.

MARGARET: (*Concerned.*) OH MY GOD, does Luther know?

PAUL: (*Nervously.*) Leo and I are meeting with him this morning.

MARGARET: Luther is going to shit!

PAUL: (*Hesitates; handing her the document.*) Here's the draft we're presenting. (*Margaret is reading the document.*)

PAUL: (*Continues.*) Please tell me if there's anything I should add.

MARGARET: (*While reading.*) Fuck! So, you can definitely tie Mr. Gilreath to this Panamanian company?

PAUL: Yes.

MARGARET: And this company is not listed as a related party?

PAUL: No. It's not mentioned anywhere in the financials.

MARGARET: This is interesting … Oh, you misspelled beneficiaries.

PAUL: I'm a horrible speller. Could you cross it out and correct it?

(*Paul tries to hand her a pen.*)

MARGARET: Let me see the equity folder.

PAUL: Could you make the correction …?

(Margaret looks first on the desk and then in audit trunk.)

PAUL: *(Continues.)* Leo must have the folder … Could you make the …

(Paul is chasing Margaret around the room.)

MARGARET: You know Luther's daughter is dating Mr. Gilreath's son!

PAUL: Let's finish proofing my work paper … Here's a pen.

MARGARET: I can't believe this.

PAUL: How do you spell beneficiaries?

(Margaret finally takes the pen and makes the correction.)

PAUL: *(Continues.)* Thank you.

MARGARET: Mr. Gilreath would have had to file a report with the SEC explaining his reasons for cashing in a large bundle of stock options. You need to get a copy of that report.

PAUL: Could you write that on the bottom of the page?

(Margaret begins writing.)

PAUL: *(Continues.)* Oh good. Thanks. *(Looking over her shoulder.)* I left the date off. Could you ... Thanks again.

MARGARET: It's a good thing y'all caught this before releasing the financial statements. The SEC would be all over your asses!

PAUL: Margaret, with Mr. Gilreath being a close friend of Luther's, we really need to keep this quiet.

MARGARET: God, he's going to have a fucking aneurysm.

PAUL: You've been a big help … I hope someday our friendship will be restored.

(Margaret picks up the rose and hands it back to Paul. On her way out the door, she grabs the bottle of vodka.)

PAUL: (*Continues. After she's gone, sarcastically.*) Try
      not to drink it all before lunch.
      *(Paul two-hole-punches the top of the document and
      attaches it into the middle of a folder. Leo enters.
      Paul is jumpy.)*
LEO: I thought you jumped ship.
PAUL: No.
      *(Leo gets his first clear view of the "new" Paul. Leo
      notices Paul's matching tie and socks.)*
LEO: Goddamn. (*Pause.*) Little boy blue. On Friday did
      you go home and lie down?
PAUL: No. When I got there your wife called. I spent the
      afternoon with Diane.
LEO: Did Diane sit on your dick and do a 360? That
      woman is so limber.
PAUL: Surprisingly so.
      *(Paul picks up a different folder than the one he
      inserted the new document in.)*
LEO: If she wants, Diane can make me come in fifteen
      seconds or thirty minutes. Total control. She has this
      trick ---
PAUL: Sorry to hear about your separation.
LEO: Who have you been talking to?
PAUL: (*Quickly.*) Diane and I are friends. That's all.
      Nothing else. Just friends.
LEO: Girlfriends? … Stay out of my fucking business.
      *(Pause. Paul reaches into his audit bag and pulls out
      a bundle of mail.)*
PAUL: (*Handing Leo the bundle.*) Leo … Diane did ask
      me to give you this … It's your mail.
      (Leo knocks the mail out of Paul's hand.)
LEO: You flaming little faggot
      (Pause.)
PAUL: I've received all my confirmations. (*Hands Leo
      the folder.*) You need to sign off on these pages. I've
      tabbed the first and the last page.

(Leo begins initialing the bottom of each page. _
PAUL: (*Continues.*) Aren't you going to review the work
       papers?
LEO: No. I'm sure you've over audited. *(Throwing the
       folder.)* Here.
PAUL: (*Reaching for the folder that he had placed the
       document in earlier.)* Wait. I also have the accounts-
       receivable folder.
LEO: Give it to me.
       *(Leo begins initialing pages. Paul grows
       increasingly nervous.)*
LEO: (*Continues.*) All their major customers responded?
PAUL: Yes.
       (Leo stops and examines a work paper.)
LEO: Paul.
       (Pause.)
PAUL: What?
LEO: Come over here!
       (Paul slowly crosses to Leo.)
LEO: (*Continues.*) This customer has a cash flow problem.
       They recently laid off a thousand employees.
PAUL: I know. I considered it when I was calculating the
       allowance for doubtful accounts. They owe a
       substantial amount for outstanding invoices over a
       hundred and twenty days. Since they are a major
       customer, I'll also note it in my going-concern
       evaluation.
       (Pause.)
LEO: (*Handing the folder to Paul.)* Here.
PAUL: (*Relieved.*) Thank you, Leo.
LEO: You're welcome, shithead … Where the hell is
       Greg?
PAUL: In Margaret's office.
       (Leo picks up the phone and dials.)
LEO: (*On phone.*) Tell Greg to get his ass in here!

PAUL: You should be nice to Margaret now that she's a
     manager.
LEO: Go get Luther's golden boy!
PAUL: You think he's the next superstar?
LEO: Yeah.
PAUL: Hah!
LEO: Jealous of your little buddy?
PAUL: No. Go look at Greg's work papers. Try to make
     any sense out of them. Ten years from now, you can
     pick up any of my work papers and you'll know
     exactly what I did and the results … You sent him
     back to Mason Industries to investigate those
     differences. Hah! The explanations he came back
     with are nonsense! The controller was toying with
     him and Greg's clueless. *(Pause; looking at the
     door.)* And Greg doesn't pay attention to anything.
     Did you ever notice, he's either staring out the
     window or looking down at his "nice" shoes? Every
     hour, you're lucky to get ten minutes of work out of
     him. After ten minutes, he's useless. Unable to
     sustain. The next superstar. Hah!
LEO: Greg knows how to play the game.
PAUL: Leo. Leo. What about you? When will you
     become partner? Why aren't you the next David
     McClain?
LEO: Because I don't give a fuck.
PAUL: Do you have any job offers?
LEO: I receive calls every day.
PAUL: Then why are you still here?
LEO: I'll never work on another audit with you again.
PAUL: That's not an option.
     (Greg enters.)
LEO: *(To Greg.)* Don't make me have to chase you down.
GREG: I was busy.

LEO: (*Handing Greg a stack of papers.*) Add this to what
     you're doing. Proof the footnotes and then I want you
     to foot the financials.
     (*Referring to Paul's earlier comment.*) … Nice shoes.
GREG: Thanks.
PAUL: I have to leave by six.
LEO: I wouldn't make plans.
PAUL: You'll manage without me this one time.
LEO: I'll remember this.
     (*Leo exits the room.*)
PAUL: (*To Greg.*) I have a dinner date.
GREG: It better not be with a client.
PAUL: (*Jokingly.*) Yeah, I'm having dinner with your little
     girlfriend Pam.
     (*Paul pulls out a devotional book and opens it to a
     devotion. In silence, he reads a brief prayer. Closing
     the book.*) Good. This morning I hadn't had time for
     my daily devotion.
GREG: What are you reading?
PAUL: (*Handing Greg the book.*) You need to get a copy,
     365 *Daily Devotions*.
GREG: (*Quickly flipping through the book.*) Not any of
     that liberal crap, is it?
PAUL: No. No… It's on the Christian Coalition book list.
GREG: Good. Remember Bud, it's got to be the word.
PAUL: I am so blessed to have you in my life.
GREG: Thanks, Bud.
PAUL: You look sharp today. Is your suit tailored?
GREG: No.
PAUL: You're kidding. It's got to be.
GREG: No. Brooks Brothers.
PAUL: I thought it was tailored. It's a perfect fit. Perfect
     … You wear your clothes well. Even Kmart would
     look great on you! I wish you were my personal
     shopper.
GREG: I have some catalogs at home I'll bring you.

PAUL: Would you? … Why wasn't I born with good
    taste? You just exude class … I can't compete with
    that. *(Pause.)* Bubba, we're almost finished. Yes!
    … Leo asked me to make an archive back-up of all
    the computer disks. With most of the audit on
    computer now, we need to keep an archive copy off-
    site … Can I see your disks?
GREG: In a minute.
PAUL: Sure … Leo's in a mood again.
GREG: I noticed. *(Reaching into his audit bag and pulling
    out two disks.)* Here.
PAUL: Thanks … You're welcome to borrow my
    devotional any time.
GREG: I will.
PAUL: I love your tie. Classy.

Scene Two

MARGARET: I got your message. What's up?

LEO: (*Slightly drunk.*) That was quick.

MARGARET: I was just down the street. Greg and I had
dinner at Magnolia's.

LEO: Greg, our little boy scout.

MARGARET: Leo, what do you want?

LEO: Heard you bought a new car today.

MARGARET: A white Avalon.

LEO: Take me for a ride.

MARGARET: You really want to go?

LEO: … No.

MARGARET: Good night, Leo.

LEO: How's the gang?

MARGARET: We're all wondering who pissed in your
water bowl?
(*Margaret turns to leave.*)

LEO: Congratulations.

MARGARET: For what?

LEO: Your life in general.

MARGARET: Why didn't you study? … Leo, I
understand how you're feeling right now. I took the
fucking exam seven times!

LEO: As Diane put it on my way out the door, "It's not
that you didn't pass the exam, you failed."

MARGARET: Be happy she's gone.

LEO: She left behind over nine thousand dollars in
        Mastercard and Visa debt. Let's not forget Exxon,
        Chevron, Texaco, Sears, JC Penney's, Belk's,
        Macy's, Discover …

MARGARET: Leo.

LEO: And the fucking American Express card. Aren't you
        loving every minute of this?

MARGARET: No.

LEO: Mike and Rob came by this morning to offer their
        support. "Big boy, you'll pass next time. Christ
        sakes, law is the easiest action."

MARGARET: Don't tell me you wouldn't be doing the
        same thing if it was one of them and not you.

LEO: Shit, I'd send them a daily reminder. Write it on
        their goddamn calendar. "August 16th, are you still a
        loser today?" *(Pause.)* I know my shit! Luther can
        tell you. I have managed more audits than either
        Mike or Rob … I wasn't originally scheduled for this
        audit. But when Luther needed someone to step in, I
        said, "Yes! How soon do you need the financials?
        Sure! No problem."

MARGARET: Talk with Luther.

LEO: No … Luther hates real men. Any man who
        threatens his authority.

MARGARET: What are you going to do?

LEO: *(Sarcastically.)* Find another job. *(Holding up a
        newspaper.)* Look at all these layoffs. Lucent let go
        another five hundred people today. Do you think
        their employees had any idea when they walked in
        this morning? Hell no. That's why there's no loyalty
        anymore. *(Pause.)* Today I was turned down for the
        controller's position at a small plastics company … I
        wouldn't have taken it anyway. Not enough money.
        *(Margaret approaches Leo as if to touch him but
        backs away.)*

MARGARET: What can I do to help?

LEO: (*Mimicking her angrily.*) Ahhhh. "What can I do to
    help?" *(Pause.)* Forget about it. I screwed myself.
    Hey, you're pissing with the big boys now. *(Takes a
    drink.)* I knew they wouldn't let a woman go.
MARGARET: You're beyond salvageable.
    (Silence.)
LEO: You're right.
MARGARET: No, I'm not. *(Margaret crosses to Leo.
    This time she hugs him.)* Leo, I'm sorry.
    *(Margaret releases the embrace. Leo continues to
    make advances.)*
MARGARET: (*Continues.*) No. Never again.
LEO: Come on, I'm free!
MARGARET: No, Leo.
LEO: Honey, this is your chance.
MARGARET: Honey, I'm not interested.
LEO: (*Pinning Margaret to the floor.*) Then why did you
    come back here tonight?
MARGARET: I was concerned.
LEO: Come on. We're two of a kind. I know you've been
    trying to make me jealous with Greg. I can read your
    mind. You're not really interested in that chocolate
    ice cream.
    (Margaret kicks Leo between the legs.)
MARGARET: You're a bastard … I will never be alone
    with you again.
    *(Margaret storms out of the room. Leo curls up on
    the floor.)*

Scene Three

At rise: Projected on the conference room's white board: "Mason Industries Audit; Friday 10:45 AM; August 18, 2000; Deadline: This afternoon." Paul and Greg are working.

PAUL: (*On phone.*) I want the details at lunch … You better. OK, bye. *(To Greg.)* Another auditor gave their notice.

GREG: Who?

PAUL: Susan "I didn't read the FASB um um."

GREG: Where's she going?

PAUL: Spectrum Plastics.

GREG: Good for us.

PAUL: Did I tell you I had dinner with Pam the other night?

GREG: Did you?

PAUL: After a few drinks, she's extremely talkative. *(Silence.)* Pam said you made her cry. *(Pause.)* Did it excite you? Afterwards did you go home and beat off? … Did you? …Greg?

GREG: Yes, I did.

PAUL: After you used her, what did you tell her? … "Paul says I can't see you again."

GREG: Yeah, something like that.

PAUL: I've been thinking a lot lately about professional skepticism. *(Greg stands up to leave the room.)* Greg, I'm talking to you. Please sit down.

GREG: Fuck off.

PAUL: Pam's threatening to go to Luther.

GREG: So, what?

PAUL: … It's your career.

  (Greg sits down.)

PAUL: (*Continues.*) Good. I got your attention. Let's talk
        about professional skepticism. You're Greg, the
        auditor and I'm Paul, the client. We become good
        buddies. Best buds. You're auditing my books and
        you find discrepancies. But you think to yourself.
        Paul's my good friend. Best bud. Your judgment is
        clouded. You've lost your professional skepticism.
        This whole time, Paul, the client, is thinking of new
        ways to screw you … I just thought of another
        example. Look at us. Our company operates under a
        pyramidal structure. At the bottom of the pyramid are
        the staff accountants, like you and me. As you move
        up you have the seniors, then the managers, and
        finally the partners. At each level there are fewer and
        fewer. But we all want to be on top. Yet there are
        very few tops and a lot of bottoms. My question is,
        should we be friends with one another? Let down our
        guard?
        (Leo enters.)
PAUL: (*Continues. Looking directly at Greg.*) You told
        Pam you had found my weaknesses and you were
        trying to make my life miserable.
LEO: Paul, get to work.
PAUL: Leo, please let me finish. It's important to me.
        Thank you. There are those who believe that to
        succeed they must destroy other people. They better
        be careful they don't destroy themselves. *(Pause.)*
        Back to auditing!
LEO: (*To Paul.*) What are you working on?
PAUL: I'm going through all the final checklists.
LEO: Greg, are the financials proofed and footed?
GREG: Still working on it.
LEO: It's not a semester project. We're binding the
        financials this afternoon … Let me see what you've
        done.
GREG: Hold on.

(Leo tries to see what Greg is working on.)

LEO: What is that? *(Leo grabs Greg's folder.)* WHAT IS THIS?

GREG: Margaret asked me to do it.

LEO: You're in here working on Margaret's audit? *(Rips apart the folder.)* I want to see your goddamn timesheet. You're not charging this shit to my audit … I can't fucking believe this. Get out of my face! GET OUT! GO FIND MARGARET AND STICK YOUR HEAD UP HER ASS!

(Greg exits.)

LEO: *(Continues.)* You want to leave, too?

PAUL: No.

(Pause.)

LEO: I'll buy you lunch today.

PAUL: I've made other plans.

Scene Four

*At rise: Projected on the conference room's white
board: "Mason Industries Audit: One Week Later."
The table has been cleared. The audit trunk still sits
in the corner. Leo and Greg enter.*

LEO: (*Extremely distressed.*) Who locked the goddamn
    trunk? What's the combination?
GREG: Paul has it written in his day timer.
LEO: Fuck! Go get Paul.
    (Paul enters.)
PAUL: Good morning, Madonna!
LEO: Unlock the fucking trunk!
PAUL: Hold on. Let me find the combination. *(Paul
    starts going through his audit bag.) (To Leo.)*
    You're making me nervous. *(Working the
    combination lock.)* Nineteen … Twenty-seven …
LEO: Hurry up!
PAUL: I can't work like this!
    (Leo backs away.)
PAUL: (*Continues.*) What's going on with the Mason
    Industries audit?
LEO: Unlock the fucking trunk!
PAUL: I'm trying. Please don't yell at me … Nineteen.
    Twenty-seven. *(Opening the trunk.)* There.
    (Leo pushes Paul out of the way.)
LEO: Where are the current year work papers? This is all
    the prior year.) *(To Paul.)* Did you file away the
    current year?
PAUL: No, I haven't had a chance. Leo, what's going on?
LEO: Gilreath at Mason's was arrested yesterday
    afternoon. It's on the front page of this morning's
    Wall Street Journal.

PAUL: Why was he arrested?

LEO: Stock manipulation. A few weeks ago, you said something about their stock price.

PAUL: I don't remember. Greg audited their equity accounts.

LEO: Shit!

PAUL: (*Looking at the* Wall Street Journal.*)* It says here that their stock price rose 600 percent.

GREG: (*Grabbing the paper.)* I would have caught that.

PAUL: Maybe you weren't paying attention. *(To Leo.)* You need to talk with Luther. He probably has the current year's folders in his office.

LEO: I'm sick of this fucking job. Goddamn if I'll take any of Luther's shit.

PAUL: I bet the SEC was waiting for us to issue those financial statements. We acted with due diligence. I doubt seriously they have any grounds for criminal charges against you or Greg.

LEO: I'm giving my two-week's notice.
(Leo runs out of the room. Paul closes and locks the trunk.)

PAUL: This morning, the SEC will take custody of the audit work papers. Every procedure we performed will be scrutinized. You need to talk to Luther about your relationship with Pam.
(Margaret enters.)

PAUL: (*Continues.)* What is it the Christian Coalition guy said? They don't know they've been beaten until they're in the body bag.
(Greg races to the door.)

MARGARET: Greg.

GREG: Move out of my way.
(Greg exits.)

MARGARET: I thought you weren't going to release the financial statements.

PAUL: It wasn't my decision.

MARGARET: Luther made the decision knowing about this problem?

PAUL: You read my write-up. *(Pulling out a copy of the document.)* Here's a copy. Notice, Leo and Luther signed off on it.

MARGARET: Y'all never talked to Luther. Did you?

PAUL: I did everything I was supposed to do.

MARGARET: Oh, my God. Did Leo even read this?

PAUL: He signed off on it.

MARGARET: If he read it, he wouldn't have released the financial statements.

PAUL: Leo had a lot on his mind.

MARGARET: Because of this, Luther, Leo, and Greg will lose their jobs!
(Silence.)

MARGARET: *(Continues.)* You did it on purpose. You little maggot. If Leo wouldn't listen, why didn't you go straight to Luther?

PAUL: Why didn't we go to Luther? Your handwriting is all over it. As I recall, you told me to let Leo handle it … I'm betting you don't want to blow your chance to be partner someday. Are we singing off the same sheet of music? We've always had a *special* relationship.

MARGARET: Why did you do it?

PAUL: Because I can separate business from friendship. Because I'm a winner … I gave them the opportunity to do the right thing. I followed the audit manual and you're my witness … You know what's funny? Luther actually likes me. This morning we had a wonderful meeting … He likes me. He invited me to go play golf on Saturday. Can you see me on the golf course with Luther?

MARGARET: I'm talking with Leo.

PAUL: You're smarter than that.
(Leo enters.)

LEO: Luther took my resignation, but didn't accept my
      two-week's notice. Asked for my keys and told me to
      leave within the next fifteen minutes.
MARGARET: Leo?
PAUL: You should have let him fire you. Now you don't
      even get severance pay.
LEO: Open the trunk.
PAUL: Leo, you can't even apply for unemployment. You
      quit without cause.
LEO: I'll destroy those fucking files.
PAUL: That's just the prior year.
LEO: I don't give a fuck!
PAUL: I'm not helping you commit a crime.
      (Greg enters.)
PAUL: *(Continues. To Leo.)* Do you need anything?
MARGARET: *(To Paul.)* Haven't you done enough?
      (Handing the audit folder to Leo.) He set y'all up.
      *(Leo stops packing and looks at the folder.
      Afterwards, he slowly crosses toward Paul. Paul
      quickly picks up his audit bag and heads to the door.
      Greg blocks Paul's exit. Preparing for a fight, Leo
      removes his suit jacket. He then chases Paul around
      the table before catching him and throwing him onto
      the table. Leo jumps on top of him and starts to choke
      Paul.)*
GREG: Beat the shit out of him. Fuck him up. Fuck him
      up!
MARGARET: *(Overlapping.)* No, Leo. No! NO, LEO!
LEO: *(Overlapping.)* I could kill you. I could fucking kill
      you.
      *(Leo notices they are wearing identical ties. Leo
      releases Paul. Greg storms out of the room. Leo
      exits.)*
PAUL: Margaret, Margaret …
      *(Margaret stops at the door and picks up the equity
      folder lying on the floor. She stares at the folder.*

*After a moment, she turns and crosses to Paul.
Margaret hands him the folder.)*
PAUL: *(Continues.)* Margaret.
*(She then turns around, puts on her glasses, adjusts
her clothing, and exits the room.)*
PAUL: *(Continues.)* Margaret …
*(A bewildered Paul stands there alone. Slowly he
smiles as the lights fade to black.)*

END OF PLAY

Author Bio

James Rasheed's other plays include *August Flight, Mama Mamie's Departure, The Baristas, That's So Shannon,* and *A Series of Unfortunate Interviews.*

Contact for performances

For information regarding performing this play, please contact James Rasheed at <u>playwrightrasheed@gmail.com</u>.